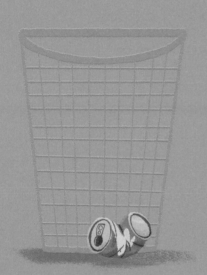

For Barb. Thanks for your
continued enthusiasm! ~ T.C.

For Olive ~ T.N.

tiger tales
5 River Road, Suite 128, Wilton, CT 06897
Published in the United States 2020
Originally published in Great Britain 2020
by Little Tiger Press Ltd.
Text copyright © 2020 Tracey Corderoy
Illustrations copyright © 2020 Tony Neal
ISBN-13: 978-1-68010-227-7
ISBN-10: 1-68010-227-3
Printed in China
LTP/1400/3127/0420
10 9 8 7 6 5 4 3 2 1

For more insight and activities,
visit us at www.tigertalesbooks.com

The Forest Stewardship Council® (FSC®) is an international,
non-governmental organization dedicated to promoting responsible
management of the world's forests. FSC operates a system of forest
certification and product labeling that allows consumers to identify
wood and wood-based products from well-managed forests.

For more information about the FSC, please visit their website at www.fsc.org

IT'S ONLY ONE!

by
Tracey Corderoy

Illustrated by
Tony Neal

tiger tales

Sunnyville was perfect.
Friendly and fun.
It twinkled with total loveliness!

But then, without thinking . . .

. . . Rhino did **this.**

But it wasn't.

BONK!

So **he** did this.

What? It's only one.

But—of course . . .

. . . it wasn't!

Penguin was **fuming**.

I **loved** those flowers!

But some **music** might cheer things up . . . .

Wrong again!
Mouse couldn't believe her EARS.

This was simply awful.

Sunnyville had lost its twinkle completely.
And now EVERYONE was grumpy!

Then Mouse had an idea!

Hmm.
I wonder . . . .

So she did this.

It was only one,
but . . . .

It smelled just like the Sunnyville
they all remembered.

Now Rhino knew **exactly** what to do.

And wrapper by wrapper . . .

flower by flower . . .

. . . Sunnyville soon twinkled brighter than ever.

And everyone LOVED it.

A note from the author, Tracey Corderoy . . .

I live in a beautiful little valley and love the big green trees and twinkling stream. We have chocolate-colored rabbits who hop through the fields, and little mice who scurry through the grass. Keeping it neat and a nice place to be means that everyone can enjoy it. In our story, Rhino drops just one small wrapper. He thinks this will be okay. But —uh-oh!— before he knows it, all his friends are doing just what **they** please, too, and boy, is it noisy and messy! This story is about thinking of others so everyone can be happy.

. . . and the illustrator, Tony Neal

Sometimes we might want to say, "It's only one!" But if we all dropped "only one" piece of trash, things would become a lot messier! Let's be clean, try to be green, and keep the places we live in looking great. We can do this by being thoughtful about our actions and the way we treat others. Let's take care of this planet we live on—we have only one!

Let's learn to be good neighbors!

Little acts of kindness make our neighborhood a better place to live. Let's try to . . .
* smile and say "hello" when we meet our friends
* treat others as we would like to be treated
* take care of the spaces we all share
* help those in need

Let's put our litter in the trash cans!

No one likes to look at garbage. It can also be smelly, and harmful to both people and animals. Let's try to . . .
* carry our litter until we find the nearest trash can
* take it home if we cannot find a trash can
* recycle our trash whenever possible

Let's make our park a happy place!

Everyone loves the park, so treat it with good care.
Let's try to . . .
* leave the flowers unpicked, so that everyone can enjoy them
* be kind and gentle to birds, squirrels, ducks, and other wildlife
* share when we play on the swings or the slide

Let's learn from each other!

I'll help my neighbors!

I won't call people names.

Let's keep the noise down!

It can be fun to scream, shout, and play music—but remember that others might prefer peace and quiet. Let's try to . . .

* be aware of other people when playing with our friends
* keep the volume low on our TVs and music systems
* tread lightly with our feet if others live below us

I'll share my toys with others!

I'll be kind!

I'll turn my music down.

I'll put my trash in the garbage can!

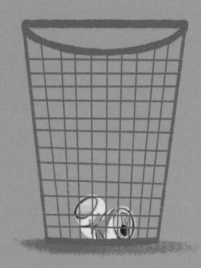
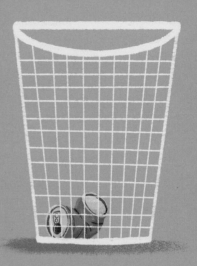
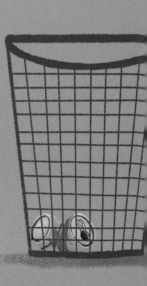